TO: NATALIE

Love,
NaNa

Need A House?
Call Ms. Mouse!

Need A House? Call Ms. Mouse!

By George Mendoza

Illustrated by Doris Susan Smith

Ms. Mouse & Co.

Builders

•

Decorators

•

Designers

Publishers · GROSSET & DUNLAP · New York
A FILMWAYS COMPANY

This one for Doris Duenewald,
who has always been my friend...

Library of Congress Catalog Card Number: 81-80884
ISBN: 0-448-16575-9
Copyright © 1981 by Grosset & Dunlap, Inc. and Librairie Ernest Flammarion.
All rights reserved.
Photogravure : Lappas-Barcelone
Printed in Belgium by Offset Printing Van den Bossche. ☒
Published simultaneously in Canada.

Henrietta's Portfolio

Squirrel's Treehouse
Trout's Paradise
Cat's Villa
Mole's Manor
Fox's Den
Rabbit's Farm
Worm's Cocoon
Bear's Cave
Lizard's Beach House
Frog's Pad
Spider's Web
Owl's Tower
Pig's Palace
Otter's Lodge
Henrietta's Hideaway

Meet Henrietta.
   Also known as Ms. Mouse.

Henrietta is a world famous decorator, which means
she is — an artist, a designer, a dreamer,
         a builder, a creator, all that and more, too.

   You may have heard about Henrietta from your
forest friends. Squirrels, rabbits, chipmunks, and all
kinds of birds know her. Even worms know about Henrietta.
   You see, Henrietta is a genius. Her head is like a
carousel whirling with colors, fabrics, and designs.
   Look at her. Always at her drawing table, always
creating for others. There she is roughing out her
schemes and themes trying to change each creature's house
from the commonplace to the extraordinary. For hours and
hours she struggles to find perfection.
   Sometimes she labors far into the night without
even thinking of nibbling on a piece of bread or cheese.

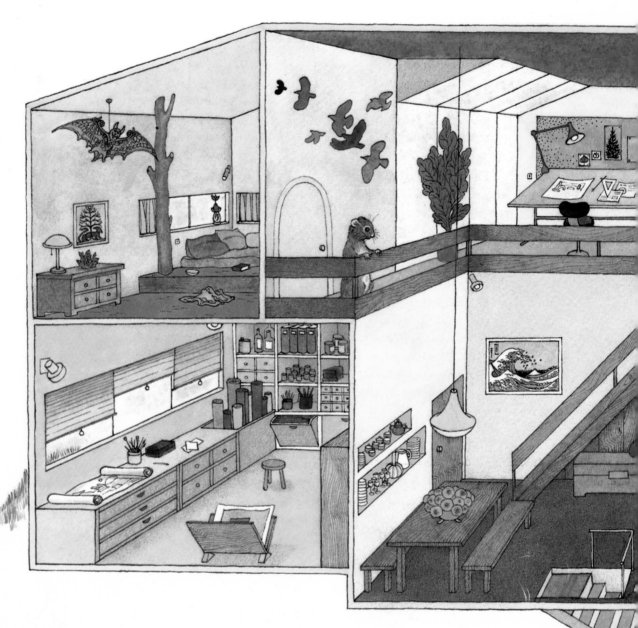

But there are so many demands upon her. So
many friends to please! Thank goodness for her faithful
little mice helpers.

Imagine, Squirrel asks Henrietta to design a
spaceship feeling in the branches of a knotty tree.

Trout, beautiful brown Trout, wants his watery underworld to resemble the lost paradise of Atlantis!

Cat, lazy Cat, purrs for lots of beds and wrap-around terraces for the sole purpose of being what cats like to be best, lazy. Better lazy as far as Henrietta is concerned than on the hunt for mice.

Mole desires a more convenient and more luxurious way up to the top of the ground.

Please, Henrietta, an end to earthy
entrances and exits for Monsieur Mole.

Fox hopes only for a comfortable den—a place to relax after a long day's running and cunning.

But Rabbit, being a most industrious farmer, asks Henrietta to decorate a hole to fill his stomach's delight. Lots of city people would like to live like Rabbit, don't you agree?

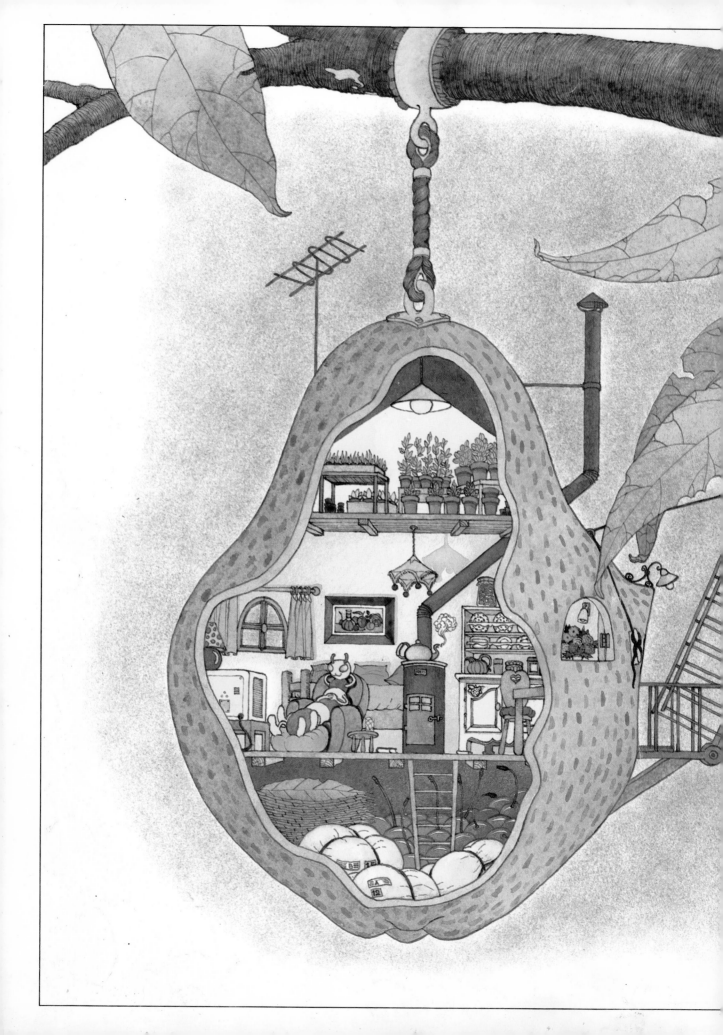

Worm achieves the very core of his dream—
thanks to Henrietta's extraordinary imagination.

Bear, old furry Bear, is so pleased with his new cozy cave, he barely goes mountain climbing anymore.

Lizard, crusty character, asks Henrietta for a splendid beach house—a place to enjoy the sun coming up and the sun going down.

Frog's pad is a leaping success. Croak! Croak!

Spider's web becomes a musical dive with a magical tuned-up beat. Beware flying gnats, moths, and flies!

Owl, night's glider under moon's eye, can finally gaze beyond the lights of this world to the farthest star.

Pig is so fussy you would think she
is the Queen of England. See what
piggy money can do!

Otter tells Henrietta: "Please build me a sturdy hunting and fishing lodge!"

As for Henrietta, she cares only for
the simple life!
What about you?